GHOST DETECTORS

One, Two, Three, Kick!

BOOK 23

BY
JAN FIELDS

ILLUSTRATED BY
DAVE SHEPHARD

Calico

An Imprint of Magic Wagon
abdopublishing.com

For all the fantastic people who edit my work and make me look so good. — JF

For Albie, for trying to hold silly poses while I draw. — DS

abdopublishing.com

Published by Magic Wagon, a division of ABDO, PO Box 398166, Minneapolis, Minnesota 55439. Copyright © 2018 by Abdo Consulting Group, Inc. International copyrights reserved in all countries. No part of this book may be reproduced in any form without written permission from the publisher. Calico™ is a trademark and logo of Magic Wagon.

Printed in the United States of America, North Mankato, Minnesota.
092017
012018

 **THIS BOOK CONTAINS RECYCLED MATERIALS**

Written by Jan Fields
Illustrated by Dave Shephard
Edited by Bridget O'Brien
Designed by Christina Doffing

Publisher's Cataloging-in-Publication Data

Names: Fields, Jan, author. | Shephard, Dave, illustrator.
Title: One, two, three, kick! / by Jan Fields; illustrated by Dave Shephard.
Description: Minneapolis, Minnesota : Magic Wagon, 2018. | Series: Ghost detectors; Book 23
Summary: Cocoa demands Malcolm and Dandy do their sneaky best to find out who or what is trying to sabotage her upcoming dance recital.
Identifiers: LCCN 2017946455 | ISBN 9781532131554 (lib.bdg.) | ISBN 9781532131653 (ebook) | ISBN 9781532131707 (Read-to-me ebook)
Subjects: LCSH: Ghost stories--Juvenile fiction. | Dance recitals--Juvenile fiction. | Sabotage--Juvenile fiction. | Humorous Stories--Juvenile fiction.
Classification: DDC [FIC]--dc23
LC record available at https://lccn.loc.gov/2017946455

Contents

Chapter 1
Basement Monster

Malcolm crept down the stairs, wincing at the strange noises.

Tap, scrape, THUMP! Tap, scrape, THUMP! Tap, scrape, THUMP!

Whether ghost or monster, something scary lurked in his basement laboratory. Maybe a ghost had come to haunt him. Maybe a monster escaped from a movie. It wouldn't be the first time.

Whatever it was, he intended to teach it not to mess with his laboratory.

Malcolm gripped the baseball bat he'd borrowed from Dad's room. He would fend off the monster until his friend Dandy could reach the Ecto-Handheld-Automatic-Heat-Sensitive-Laser-Enhanced Ghost Zapper.

Dandy pressed against his back, jumping with each *THUMP*. "Maybe we should wait upstairs," he whispered. "Until it goes away."

"That's not what Ghost Detectors do," Malcolm said. Besides, his ghost dog Spooky was in his lab. And he wasn't going to risk some monster hurting his dog.

At the bottom of the stairs, he took a breath. Then he rushed into the basement with the baseball bat over his head. "Aaaaahhhh!"

"Aaaaahhhh!" shrieked Malcolm's older sister, Cocoa. She jumped back on the floor with a *THUMP!*

Cocoa was wearing tap shoes and a black leotard. Her bright pink pants matched her bright pink lip gloss and pink streaks in her hair. She snarled at Malcolm. "You!"

"You!" he yelled back. "You were making those noises!"

He looked around the space. Someone had shoved his old desk in the corner and

tossed the beanbag chair after it to make room for two big sheets of plywood that lay on the floor like wooden rugs.

"You wrecked my laboratory!"

Cocoa scrambled up and put her hands on her hips. "You ruined my dance practice."

"This is trespassing. Get out of my lab." Malcolm pointed toward the stairs and looked to Dandy for support.

Dandy didn't notice. He walked over and flopped on the beanbag chair near the desk. He found an old cheese curl in the folds of the chair and popped it in his mouth.

"If this is your lab, then he must be your lab experiment." Cocoa sneered. "Look, nerd! You and your experiment need to clear out. Dad brought these boards down here so I can practice. You don't own the basement."

"Why don't you practice in your room?" Malcolm asked.

"Because Grandma Eunice kept yelling, 'The sky is falling!' Mom said it made her nervous. So Dad said I could practice down here."

"Fine." Malcolm stomped toward the stairs. He'd chased Cocoa out of his laboratory before. He could do it again. He just needed a plan. "Come on, Dandy."

Dandy wrestled out of the beanbag.

"Hold it! Wait a minute," Cocoa yelled. "I might have a job for you two."

"We are not interested in doing your chores," Malcolm yelled over his shoulder.

"Not my chores. I'm talking about a case, an investigation."

Malcolm turned around to see his sister smirk. Cocoa's bright pink, twisted lips

looked like two slugs waltzing. It was gross.

"I know you two are always slinking around, poking your noses where they don't belong. I need you to do that for me."

"We're listening," Malcolm said, though he was pretty sure Dandy wasn't listening. His friend was shaking the beanbag chair and eating whatever fell out.

"Someone in my dance class is trying to ruin the recital. Stuff keeps disappearing. The lights flip off and on. And at the last rehearsal, someone put gum on the stage, and we all stuck to it."

Cocoa's sneer slid off her face. She chewed some of the gloss from her lower lip. "All the dancers are getting scared. Miss Nan said if the pranks don't stop, she will cancel the recital."

Since Malcolm couldn't think of too many things worse than being stuck watching a dance recital, he couldn't see why he should help. "So?"

"So this is my big chance," Cocoa wailed, clutching her chest dramatically. "There could be a talent agent in the audience. I could be discovered! I could become a star!" She flung her arms wide.

"And I could become a lizard," Malcolm said. "But it's not likely."

Cocoa dropped her arms and leaned toward Malcolm. "You're already a lizard. Now I need you to scamper around and figure out what's going on."

Malcolm folded his arms over his chest. He and Dandy were Ghost Detectors. They had faced the scariest ghosts anyone could imagine. They certainly weren't going to

be ordered around by Cocoa, not without a sweet deal.

"Say we figure it out. What do we get?"

Cocoa glared at him. "If you don't do this, I'll tell Mom about all the sneaking around you do."

"You already do that," Malcolm said. "You put the tail in tattletale."

"I think that's a different kind of tail," Dandy said. He shook the beanbag chair some more.

"Not when the tattletale is a rat," Malcolm said, "like Cocoa."

Cocoa looked so mad Malcolm thought steam might come out of her ears. Her face turned as bright pink as her lip gloss. But she finally said, "Fine. What do you want?"

"You do my chores for a month."

"A week," Cocoa countered.

"Two weeks," Malcolm said.

"And we get a bag of cheese puffs," Dandy added. "A big one."

"It's a deal," Cocoa said. "But you two better get results. Or else."

Chapter 2
Snap to It

"You want your brother to come to dance practice?" Mom pointed at Malcolm. "This brother?"

Cocoa rolled her eyes, which had to be tough with so much eye shadow caked on them. "I only have one brother."

"Just checking." Mom looked at them suspiciously. "It's nice that you two are getting along. But I thought Malcolm could stay home and keep Grandma Eunice company."

They turned to look at Grandma Eunice. She sat on the couch in the den clutching a bowl of popcorn. She was also shouting wrong answers at a quiz show on TV. Every time the television disagreed with her, she threw popcorn at the screen.

Dandy sat on the floor next to the couch. He picked up the flung popcorn and ate it.

Even though she was older than dirt, Malcolm knew his great-grandmother only pretended to be loopy. That way she didn't have to do any chores. Plus, it meant she could do almost anything and never get in trouble. He wished he'd thought of it first.

"Grandma Eunice could come too," Cocoa said, sticking a sick smile on her face. "We can have some family bonding time. You and Dad are always talking about that."

"You know, if we take your brother, we're going to have to bring Dandy too," Mom said. "His folks don't get home for another few hours. We can't make him go home to an empty house."

Cocoa's smile wobbled as she watched Dandy eat popcorn off the floor. "That's fine. I like Dandy. And I appreciate all the support."

If she dances as badly as she lies, Malcolm thought, *the recital is doomed*.

"Pepper pots!" Grandma Eunice yelled. "Pepper pots and peas!"

"I think the answer is Washington," Dandy told her.

The game show host agreed with Dandy. Grandma Eunice threw another handful of popcorn at the television.

"Are you sure, Cocoa?" Mom asked.

Cocoa's smile wobbled even more, but she nodded. "It'll be fun."

Mom shook her head. "Fine. Let's load everyone in the car and head to rehearsal. But you all need to be on your best behavior."

"Of course," Malcolm agreed.

"Martian dance parties," Grandma Eunice yelled.

"The Revolutionary War," Dandy yelled.

It was hard to hear with all the noise. But Malcolm thought Mom might have whimpered a little.

It was Malcolm's turn to whimper as he sat squished in the back of the car. Dandy had insisted on being paid his cheese puffs up front. So he crunched happily next to Malcolm on the way to Cocoa's rehearsal.

Grandma Eunice sat on Malcolm's other side, waving at passing cars. The smell of

fake cheese mixed with Grandma Eunice's arthritis ointment stink made Malcolm queasy. Either that or the thought of watching a bunch of girls stomp around on stage was making him sick.

In the front seat, Cocoa slathered on hand lotion. It added a flowery scent to the battling smells in the car.

When they finally reached the theater, Malcolm was feeling a little wobbly. Cocoa dragged him aside as soon as he got out of the car. "You better find out who's doing this."

"I know, I know," Malcolm said. He wrinkled his nose as the smell of cotton candy lip gloss made his stomach roll. "Or else."

"Once we're inside," she growled, "pretend you don't know me."

Malcolm pulled away from her slimy hand. "I wish."

Pushing Grandma Eunice's wheelchair, Mom rolled by them. Grandma Eunice winked at Malcolm and sang show tunes loudly while Mom shushed her.

Malcolm didn't mind the screeching sound. It kept Cocoa from talking to him. In fact, she ran ahead of all of them. "Remember," she yelled back. "Pretend you don't know me."

"So much for family bonding," Mom muttered.

Dandy stopped beside Malcolm, still crunching through the cheese puffs. "What do we do now?"

Malcolm hitched his backpack of Ghost Detecting supplies up on his shoulder. He knew there probably wasn't a ghost in the

theater. But he could always hope for the best. "We find out what's going on. And we stop it."

Inside the small theater, rows of red-padded seats faced the stage. The first row was full of kids in dance gear. Stray parents sat in the back two rows. Malcolm was surprised to see that some of the dancers were boys.

A thin woman with a tight, round bun on her head stood on the stage and peered down at everyone. She clapped her hands and shouted, "Quiet. I will have perfect quiet at rehearsals."

"Won't you need music?" Grandma Eunice asked. "Plus, if you're going to keep clapping, it's not going to be all that quiet."

"Don't forget the shouting," Dandy said.

"Stop mentioning it," Mom said.

The dance teacher's eyes narrowed. She clapped again. "I will have quiet in the audience or the audience will leave!" She pointed at Cocoa. "Now, if you don't mind joining the others, we can begin."

"Yes, Miss Nan."

Cocoa gave Malcolm the stink eye. Then she ran to the front and flopped in the last seat. As soon as she did, the front row seats snapped shut on the dancers. The seats shoved the dancers' heads against their knees.

"Stop this!" the teacher yelled as she clapped some more. "Stop this at once!"

If the theater seats heard her, they didn't seem to care. If anything, they tightened on the squirming dancers.

Malcolm took one look and grinned at Dandy. "I smell a ghost!"

Dandy sniffed his hand and shrugged. "All I smell is cheese."

Chapter 3
Not Fair!

The dancers yelled for help. Malcolm and Dandy ran to the front and grabbed Cocoa's hands. Her hands were still slimy with lotion. But they pulled until she popped out of the seat. As soon as she did, the other seats popped open.

The teacher pointed at the boys. "You two! Stop playing around. It is time for rehearsal, not for little boys to play tricks."

"Us?" Malcolm yelped. That was so unfair. He looked at his best friend. Dandy

just shrugged and pulled the half empty cheese puffs bag out of his backpack.

"What are you doing!" the dance teacher shouted. "Get that food out of this theater!"

Mom left Grandma Eunice in the middle of the aisle and rushed over to Malcolm and Dandy. "Why don't you boys take Grandma Eunice for a walk? I'm sure that will make things easier for everyone."

"We didn't make the seats fold up," Malcolm said. "We weren't near them."

His mom gave him a tired smile. "I know. I appreciate your help."

Malcolm and Dandy began pushing the wheelchair. Dandy left orange stains on the handles. He also left a trail of puffs from the bag that dangled from his fingers.

They pushed through the double doors at the back of the theater and into the foyer.

"How are we supposed to investigate from out here?" Malcolm grumbled.

"Investigate?" Grandma Eunice asked. "What's the caper?"

"Someone is trying to wreck the recital," Dandy told her. He licked orange powder from his fingers.

"Someone or something," Malcolm said. "The Ghost Detectors are going to figure out what is going on and stop it!"

Grandma Eunice grinned and rubbed her hands together. "Great. Then we should start by checking backstage."

"How do we do that?" Malcolm asked. "We were just thrown out."

Grandma Eunice flapped a hand at the door behind them. "Don't mind the dance teacher, boys. I think her bun is twisted too tight. We can get to the backstage area that

way." She pointed toward a small hallway. "Tallyho!"

"I thought this was the way to the bathrooms," Malcolm said. He and Dandy pushed the chair down the hall.

"It is. And the dressing rooms and backstage." Grandma Eunice sighed. "When I was young, I performed in musicals here. I was known for my silver voice."

"Was it haunted way, way, way back then?" Dandy asked.

Grandma Eunice poked him. "It wasn't that long ago!"

"Was it haunted?" Malcolm asked. "Strange happenings? Cold spots? Scary noises?"

"Not a bit. The theater was full of the sound of singing." She began to sing loudly about living hills and music.

Malcolm didn't know what a silver voice sounded like. But Grandma Eunice's wailing reminded him of someone poking a cat with a silver stick. Malcolm finally understood where Cocoa got her singing voice. The howling made Dandy drop his cheese puffs and cover his ears.

"Grandma Eunice," Malcolm said. "Will you hold the specter detector? We need to listen for the beeping." He was desperate to get his great-grandmother to stop singing. Even if that meant letting her help.

"Of course," she said. "Fork it over."

Malcolm dug the Ecto-Handheld-Automatic-Heat-Sensitive-Laser-Enhanced Specter Detector out of his backpack. He handed it to his great-grandmother. She grinned and held it up.

Bleep, bleep, bleep, bleep!

"The ghost is close," Malcolm said. He worried about Grandma Eunice singing again. He added, "If we're really quiet, maybe we can sneak up on it."

"Won't it hear the bleeping?" Dandy asked.

"As long as it doesn't hear singing," Malcolm said, "we should be fine. We don't want to scare it away."

"I don't think that will be a problem," Grandma Eunice said. She pointed the specter detector toward the end of the hallway. "I'm guessing that's the ghost."

Malcolm looked where Grandma Eunice pointed at the end of the hall. A tall woman with a tight bun on her head floated above the floor. She glared in their direction.

She had her hands on her hips and her bony elbows high. She looked exactly

like Cocoa's dance teacher, except Cocoa's teacher couldn't float. And you couldn't see through her.

"What do you think you're doing here?" the ghost demanded. "I never let noisy little boys in my rehearsals! Little boys always make trouble and noise. So much noise!"

Giselle.

"Hey," Malcolm complained. "I'm not the noisy one!"

"Silence!" The ghost clapped exactly like Cocoa's dance teacher. Only when the ghost clapped her hands, the lights went out, plunging them into darkness.

That's when the screaming started.

Chapter 4
Shuffle Off to Where?

The screaming from inside the theater didn't last long. Malcolm figured the teacher didn't like screaming much either.

Malcolm fumbled in his backpack until he found his flashlight. He grabbed it and shone it around the hall. The ghost was gone.

Dandy stood beside Grandma Eunice's wheelchair with his finger up his nose. He left behind an orange smear that Malcolm tried not to look at too long.

A bright light flashed in Malcolm's eyes, nearly blinding him. He staggered back a step or two.

"I thought this might happen," Grandma Eunice crowed. "That's why I brought my Blazing Atomic Flashlight. I ordered it from the TV. Don't tell your mom. I used her credit card. Isn't it a doozy? It should be a big help in our work."

"It's great," Malcolm said. "Can you shine it somewhere else?" Then as he tried to blink away the spots in front of his eyes, he realized what Grandma Eunice had said. "Our work?"

"Yeah, detecting ghosts."

Malcolm took a deep breath. He looked at Dandy, but his friend was staring at his finger. No help there. "Look, there are only two Ghost Detectors, Dandy and me."

She rolled her chair closer to him, and shone the light back in his eyes. "I've helped. You know I have."

"Yes, but you're . . ." He shielded his eyes, trying to think of how best to finish the sentence. Old? Loony? He finally chose, "Support staff."

Grandma Eunice thought about that for a moment, then nodded. "Vital support staff. With a flashlight."

"Why don't I have a flashlight?" Dandy asked.

"Because you didn't bring an equipment bag. If we are done with question time, can we go find the ghost?" Malcolm asked. "Because it needs zapping."

He reached into the backpack to grab the Ecto-Handheld-Automatic-Heat-Sensitive-Laser-Enhanced Ghost Zapper.

The door leading to the backstage area slammed open. A line of tap dancers shuffled out. Their tiny steps rung on the hard tile floor of the hallway. *Tippity, tippity, tippity, tap.* They shuffled toward the dressing rooms. *Tippity, tippity, tippity, tap.*

"That is one weird dance," Dandy said.

"Looks like a train," Grandma Eunice sang out. "Choo choo!"

Cocoa reached out to grab Malcolm. "This is no dance. When the lights went out, someone tied all our shoelaces together."

Malcolm looked down at the dancers' feet. The thin laces of each pair of shiny, black tap shoes were tied in a clump of knots. The dancers could only take tiny steps. "Wow."

Cocoa gave Malcolm a shake. "Did you do it?"

"Do what?" Malcolm asked.

"Maybe she wants to know if you did the choo-choo dance," Dandy said.

Cocoa growled at Dandy, then gave Malcolm another shake. "Did you turn off the lights and tie our shoes together?"

"No," Malcolm said, pulling his arm loose before Cocoa made his brain rattle. "I was out in the hall trying to find a way in.

So I could solve your mystery. It's not my fault your teacher threw us out."

"Miss Nan thinks you two turned off the lights," Cocoa said. "She was yelling in the dark about the little boys making trouble."

"No fair! The ghost said we were noisy boys too." He pointed at Grandma Eunice. "She's the noisy one."

"It's true," Grandma Eunice said. "I am."

"I don't care," Cocoa snapped. "You find out who is doing all this. And stop them."

"We're on the job," Grandma Eunice sang out.

Cocoa groaned. Then she turned and dragged the other dancers into the dressing room. As the door swung closed behind her, the lights snapped back on in the hallway.

Malcolm turned to Dandy and Grandma Eunice. "Did you guys notice how much the ghost looked like Miss Nan?"

Dandy was trying to pull a cheese curl from his hair. "Huh?"

"It's the bun head," Grandma Eunice said. "It makes them all look alike."

"Maybe," Malcolm said, but he wasn't sure. Maybe the ghost wasn't haunting the theater. Maybe it was haunting Miss Nan.

Chapter 5
The Only One

Malcolm looked over at the dressing room doors. "It will probably take awhile to untie those knots. We should look around backstage."

"Good idea. That ghost has to be around here somewhere." Grandma Eunice waved the specter detector toward the backstage door. "Let's move it!"

"How come we have to push?" Malcolm asked. "You zip around the house and even do wheelies in this thing."

"I can't afford to get tired out," Grandma Eunice said. "In case we have trouble later." She gave him a bright smile.

Malcolm didn't know if he believed that. He sighed. He got behind the wheelchair and pushed. Grandma Eunice was pretty heavy for a little old lady.

He looked over at Dandy, who had gotten the cheese curl out of his hair. He was looking it over closely. Malcolm cleared his throat. "You going to help?"

"Sure." Dandy took one more look at the cheese curl, shrugged, and popped it in his mouth. Then he walked over and grabbed the stage door. "You can go through now."

Malcolm gave him the stink eye. "Thanks a bunch, pal."

"You're welcome," Dandy said politely as he held open the door.

Malcolm heaved the chair through the narrow door while Grandma Eunice launched into another song. The door led to the cluttered area behind the stage curtains. Not much light brightened the area. Many of the stored props were little more than dark blobs in the shadows.

"We should be stealthy," Malcolm said.

"Good idea," Grandma Eunice said. "I'll be quiet as a mouse."

Though Dandy was finally helping push, they rolled slowly through the space behind the curtain. Now and then the wheelchair brushed against the heavy, velvet curtain with a creepy shushing sound.

Up ahead, Malcolm spotted the back of a tight bun. "Right there!" he yelped.

Grandma Eunice switched on her flashlight. She pointed it, along with the

specter detector, at the person turning around. Miss Nan blinked against the light, then raised her hands. "Don't shoot!"

"Huh?" the Ghost Detectors said all together.

Malcolm looked at the specter detector clutched in Grandma Eunice's hand. He guessed it did look like a ray gun.

"Um, don't worry," he said. Malcolm tugged the specter detector out of Grandma Eunice's grasp and held it behind his back. "It's just a toy."

"A toy!" the dance teacher snapped. "What are you doing back here with toys? I told you to stay out of my theater during rehearsal!" She pointed toward the door.

"Nobody's rehearsing," Malcolm said. "They're all in the dressing room untying knots."

"A childish prank," Miss Nan said. "The kind of prank little boys like to play. This is why I do not let little boys in my rehearsals." She folded her arms over her chest.

Malcolm was getting tired of being blamed for things he didn't do. "Cocoa said weird things happened at the last rehearsal too, and we weren't there."

Miss Nan narrowed her eyes. "But you are here today. Little boys always make trouble. Always so noisy."

Dandy spoke up then. "Hey, that's what the other one said."

"What other one?" Miss Nan demanded.

"The other dance teacher."

Miss Nan turned red in the face and she bellowed, "There is no other dance teacher!"

"You would say that!" Everyone turned at the sound of the new voice. The ghost

with the tight bun floated at the edge of one of the curtains. "You always acted like you were the only one!"

Miss Nan's face turned very pale as she stared at the floating specter. "Penny?" she whispered just before she fainted.

Chapter 6
Battle of the Bun Heads

D andy fanned Miss Nan with the empty cheese puffs bag. Bits of cheese powder rained down on the teacher.

Malcolm rooted in his bag for his water bottle. All he could remember about people fainting on TV was that they needed water.

Grandma Eunice leaned forward and stared at the teacher. "What a wienie," she scoffed. "Fainting at her first ghost."

Malcolm finally found his water bottle. He wasn't sure if he was supposed to pour

the water on the teacher. He started to uncap the bottle. Miss Nan's eyes popped open. "What was that?" she whispered.

"A ghost," Grandma Eunice said. "We see them all the time. Of course, we're professionals."

"We see them," Dandy agreed. "But that doesn't mean we like them."

Miss Nan shook her head. "I must be dreaming. I'm having a bad dream about the rehearsal."

"She never could handle an emergency." Everyone looked sharply toward the floating ghost. Malcolm had forgotten she was still there. "You know Miss Nan?"

"I would hope so," the ghost said. "She's my sister."

"Aha!" Malcolm said. "I knew they looked alike!"

"Penny?" Miss Nan's voice shook. "It can't be you."

"Of course it can," the ghost said. She stuck her face close to her sister. Miss Nan looked almost as pale as the ghost. "Don't I look like me?"

"I don't remember you being so pale," Miss Nan said. "And floaty."

The ghost huffed. "Well, I don't remember you being so wrinkly. We all change."

"She's the one who has been doing all the pranks," Malcolm insisted. "But don't worry. We can put a stop to that."

"Not likely!" The ghost zipped around. "No noisy little boy is going to stop me."

"Why are you ruining my rehearsals?" Miss Nan asked. "We're sisters. We ran the dance school together. Why do you want to ruin everything now?"

The ghost swooped into her sister's face again. "Because you're doing it all WRONG!"

Miss Nan scrambled to her feet. "No, I'm not!"

"Are too!"

"Am not!"

Malcolm sometimes had arguments exactly like this with Cocoa. He knew it could go on all night. So, he shouted, "Excuse me?"

Both teachers turned sharply to face him.

"Miss Penny?" he said. "What is Miss Nan doing wrong?"

The ghost swooped close to him and poked him in the chest. "She lets noisy little boys into the rehearsal."

"That wasn't my idea," Miss Nan said.

"You even put noisy boys in the recital."

"Those are dancers!" Miss Nan insisted.

The ghost roared. "No noisy boys in the theater. No noisy boys dancing. You are doing it all wrong." She swooped back over. "You let the dancers chew gum! I never let dancers chew gum."

"Only in practice," Miss Nan said. "Never in recital."

"You let them sit around in chairs."

Miss Nan waved her hands. "I wanted to talk to them."

The ghost folded her arms over her chest. "I always made them sit in a circle on the floor when I talked. And I cannot believe you let them wear tap shoes with laces. This isn't a basketball game! Buckles. They should wear buckles!"

The ghost zipped around her sister. Then she shrieked. "What's on your clothes?"

"On my clothes?" Miss Nan squinted at her leotard. "I don't see anything."

The ghost pointed, her mouth hanging open in horror. "There! There!" Malcolm saw specks of cheese puff on the teacher's clothes. He didn't think it would be helpful for Miss Nan to see it.

"Now you're just trying to make me look for something that isn't there. You were always trying to make me look bad," Miss Nan said. "But you're the one being silly!"

Her sister's mouth dropped open, and her eyes bugged out. "Silly? You're calling me silly? I'll show you, Nan Spinster. I'll show you."

With a whoosh that sent the curtains flapping, the ghost disappeared. But Malcolm had a feeling she was going to be back. And they weren't going to like it.

Chapter 7

To Zap or Not to Zap

When the ghost disappeared, Miss Nan's legs wobbled. Malcolm and Dandy helped her over to a chair.

"I can't believe it," Miss Nan said softly. "My sister is haunting me."

"Don't worry," Grandma Eunice said. "The Ghost Detectors will take care of this."

Those are my lines, Malcolm thought as he frowned at his great-grandmother. He rooted in his backpack and pulled out the ghost zapper. "We'll zap her!"

Miss Nan looked at the ghost zapper. "With bug spray?"

"This isn't bug spray," Malcolm said. Though he had to admit, it did look like bug spray. "This is the Ecto-Handheld-Automatic-Heat-Sensitive-Laser-Enhanced Ghost Zapper. We've used it on previous cases. It works."

Miss Nan didn't look happy. "Will it hurt her?"

"Hurt her?" Malcolm thought about it. The ghosts he zapped sort of melted into a puddle of purple goo. *Did it hurt?* He wasn't sure. "It gets rid of the ghost. Isn't that what's important?"

"I guess," Miss Nan said, but she still didn't look happy.

The door from the hallway swung open, letting in light and dancers. "Our knots are

all untied," Cocoa sang out. "We're ready for rehearsal."

Miss Nan looked at the ghost zapper one more time, then clapped and said, "Okay, dancers. Let's line up!"

As the dancers passed, Cocoa grabbed Malcolm's shirt. "There better not be any more problems, creep!"

She let go to follow the dancers, and Malcolm glared after her. He didn't know why Miss Nan acted so funny about zapping her sister. He'd zap his in a heartbeat.

The dancers lined up, and Miss Nan started the music. Malcolm winced. It was Cocoa's favorite boy band, Lou-Nye-Ben.

Malcolm was sure the awful music must be another prank by the ghost. But Miss Nan just counted out loud as the dancers began to shuffle their feet and tap their toes.

Then with a screech, the music changed. A song blared out about singing in the rain. The dancers stopped and looked at Miss Nan. "I don't understand," she said. "I don't even have that song in my playlist."

"You should," an eerie voice wailed. "You know it was my favorite! Now dance!"

"Is that part of the song?" one of the dancers yelled as the music grew louder and louder.

Another dancer clapped her hands over her ears. "It's too loud!"

"Dance!" the voice wailed. "You wanted to dance, didn't you?"

"Stop it!" Miss Nan yelled back. She stamped her foot. "Penny Spinster, you stop this right now."

The music stopped. The ghost appeared right in front of Miss Nan. "Make me!"

The ghost stuck her fingers in her mouth and stretched it. Her face stretched more and more. Her eyes bugged out.

At the sight of the floating ghost making faces, the dancers screamed. They ran for the steps leading down from the stage. The only dancer left was Cocoa. She scowled at Malcolm. "You're going to get it!"

Chapter 8
My Way or No Way

Miss Nan walked through the ghost. "Wait! We still have rehearsal!"

The dancers didn't wait. They rushed through the rows of seats and out the doors. The moms from the back rows hurried out with them. The doors swung shut on an empty audience.

Miss Nan yelled into the air. "Now look at what you've done!"

One door at the back of the theater opened, and Mom walked in. "Why did

everyone rush outside?" she asked. "I was talking on my phone, and they nearly ran me over."

"It was another prank." Cocoa stomped off the stage. "And it ruined rehearsal."

Mom looked at Malcolm, raising her eyebrows. He flung his arms open. "It wasn't me! Why does everyone blame me?"

"You did make a stink bomb once," Dandy said.

Mom held up her hand. "It doesn't matter. Let's go home. Will you be having rehearsal tomorrow, Miss Nan?"

"Yes. We must. We will," Miss Nan said quietly. "Please bring the noisy boys."

Mom's mouth actually hung open at that. "You want Malcolm and Dandy here during rehearsal?"

"No!" a voice called out.

"Yes!" Miss Nan said.

"No!"

"Yes!"

"We might as well go, Mom," Malcolm said. "They can do that all day. Dandy and I will bring Grandma Eunice. We'll go out the stage door and meet you outside."

"Fine," Mom said. She still looked confused.

"I'll get my stuff from the dressing room," Cocoa said. She herded the boys and Grandma Eunice into the hall. "You were supposed to stop the problem."

Malcolm stopped pushing the chair. "I will. Give me time."

"Time, time, time," Grandma Eunice sang out. "Time for a snack!"

"Oh, I love that one." Dandy sang the rest of the jingle along with her. "Take time

for a crunch, time for a munch, time for a puff of cheese!"

Cocoa groaned and marched off down the hall, muttering about her family.

"I wish I had more cheese puffs," Dandy said. "I'm hungry."

"You smeared cheese goo all over the theater," Malcolm said. He started pushing the chair again. "You even dumped some on Cocoa's teacher."

"Yeah," Dandy said. "I guess it's a good thing she didn't see it. Oh wait, there's a puff." Then he darted out from around the chair and dashed down the hall to pick up one of the puffs he'd dropped earlier.

"I like that boy," Grandma Eunice said. "It's like hanging out with Hansel. We know we'll always find our way back."

Malcolm leaned into the chair to get it rolling again. He thought about what Dandy had said. It was a good thing Miss Nan didn't see the cheese stain. She probably would have flipped just like her sister did. That ghost sure hated cheese puff powder.

Then he grinned. He had a great idea!

Chapter 9
The Power of the Puff

In the car on the way to rehearsal the next day, Malcolm sulked. "I don't see why Dandy couldn't come today."

"Because Miss Nan doesn't seem to like noisy boys. I decided to bring just you," Mom said. "I know Dandy's your friend. But we need to get through this last rehearsal without a catastrophe."

"Sure." Malcolm slumped in his seat. He had his Ghost Detecting tools, but he didn't like working without his best friend.

Mom frowned in the rearview mirror. "Why do we need the cheese puffs again?"

"It's to keep the dancers from getting hungry," Malcolm said.

"They're for the party after rehearsal," Cocoa said.

"Puffy, fluffy, cheesy chow," Grandma Eunice sang out.

"So which is it?" Mom asked. "Rehearsal party or snacks to keep the dancers from getting hungry?"

"Snack," Cocoa said.

"Party," Malcolm said.

Mom frowned so hard her eyebrows almost crossed in the middle. "You two better not be playing a trick on Miss Nan. This recital has been in enough trouble."

"It's about to get a lot better," Malcolm said. "I promise."

When they got to the theater, they found all the other moms crowded around the stage. "What was that thing yesterday?" one mom shouted.

"It scared me so bad my hair went gray," another mom said.

"She probably just ran out of hair dye," Grandma Eunice said. That's when Mom suggested Grandma Eunice have some cheese puffs, right now!

"That was just a test of a new dance instruction app," Miss Nan explained. "It's a holographic dance teacher. It still has some bugs." She clapped her hands. "But let's get rehearsal started."

The moms grumbled a little, but they filed back to their seats. Mom took Grandma Eunice's wheelchair handles. "You should come with me today."

"But Malcolm needs me!" Grandma Eunice insisted.

"Not this time." She pointed at Malcolm. "Stay out of trouble."

Malcolm tried on his most innocent smile. He didn't think it worked very well because Mom still looked suspicious.

Miss Nan called the dancers up on stage and held up a wastepaper basket. "Everyone spit out your gum, please. Then sit on the floor in a circle."

Malcolm figured Miss Nan was trying to keep the ghost happy. Then they could get through rehearsal. He had his own plan. He grabbed bags of cheese puffs from the Spiffy Mart sack. Malcolm began pouring them out in a big circle around the stage.

Soon he had a huge circle of puffy orange. As he shook the last of the crunchy puffs

from the bag, Malcolm grinned. "Now for the secret weapon." He pulled the ghost zapper out of his backpack and waited.

On the stage, the dancers had lots of questions. Some raised their hands. Most shouted.

"Dance now," Miss Nan said. "Questions later."

The dancers still shouted.

"Quiet!"

The command seemed to come from all around them. Malcolm tightened his grip on the ghost zapper. The ghost appeared near the aisle and zoomed toward the stage.

"Stop chattering like noisy boys," the ghost demanded.

Malcolm groaned. "Why is everyone picking on boys? Some of the dancers are boys!"

The ghost slammed to a stop at the circle of cheese puffs. Her pale face wrinkled.

"What is that awful smell?" She pointed at the puffs. "Junk food in the theater! Never!"

With the ghost hanging in the air, Malcolm pointed the ghost zapper at her. But before he could zap her, the ghost disappeared with a pop.

"Was that the app again?" one of the dancers asked.

Before Miss Nan could answer, a howling wind swept down the theater aisles. It swirled around the stage, picking up the cheese curls and blowing them around, faster and faster.

The dancers screamed and covered their eyes. A tornado of dusty cheese puff bits pelted them.

When the wind stopped, every dancer was totally orange. Miss Nan was orange. Malcolm was orange. Even the moms at the back of the theater were coughing from the fake cheese in the air.

"Not cool!" Cocoa said. She pointed at Malcolm. "You're going to get it!"

That was the last Malcolm heard. Miss Nan shouted, "Just another little prank, everyone. Dancers, off to the dressing rooms to wash up." The teacher looked out at the audience. "We'll be taking a short break."

Still coughing, the moms headed outside where the air didn't smell of fake cheese. As Mom wheeled her out the door, Grandma Eunice sang, "Wheeee!"

When the parents and dancers were gone, Miss Nan yelled from the stage. "Are you trying to ruin everything?"

The ghost swooped through the theater again, rushing toward Miss Nan. "Yes!"

This time Malcolm didn't wait. He squeezed the trigger on the ghost zapper. But the spray of purple goo missed the ghost as she swooped by the teacher. Instead it splattered Miss Nan.

Malcolm kept zapping, but he missed the ghost every time. The purple goo mixed with the orange puff powder. Reddish-brown strings hung from the curtains and dripped from the lights. One long strand even hung from Miss Nan's nose.

The ghost laughed wildly. "No more trouble from you, noisy boy!" The ghost swooped for Malcolm. She reached for him with fingers bent like claws.

He held up the ghost zapper. He couldn't miss this time. He squeezed the trigger.

Nothing happened. The ghost zapper was stuck!

With a cackle, the ghost rushed closer and closer.

Bam!

Cocoa had stepped around Malcolm and smacked the ghost with a bag of cheesy puffs.

The ghost shrieked as the puffs passed through her. She zoomed away from them, batting at the orange bits that seemed to cling to her.

Malcolm stared at his sister in shock.

Cocoa yelled after the ghost. "He's a creep and a pest and a nerd, but he's my brother. No one messes with him but me!"

Chapter 10
Sisters Forever!

The ghost hung in the air on the other side of the stage, brushing away cheese puffs. Cocoa glared at Malcolm. "This does not mean we're friends."

He shuddered. "Definitely not."

Malcolm turned the ghost zapper around to figure out why it didn't fire. Then he found his answer. The nozzle was clogged with a cheese puff and zapper goo mixture.

He wiped at the mess. He had to fix the zapper before the ghost attacked again.

Miss Nan stomped across the stage toward the ghost. She left drops of brown goo as she walked. "What do you want? I made the kids spit out their gum. I made them sit in a circle."

"They were noisy," the ghost said. "We never let them be noisy before. And you are letting noisy boys dance."

"We never let them be attacked by ghosts before either," Miss Nan said, glaring at the ghost. "And the boys are very good dancers. You would know that if you watched them instead of trying to ruin everything."

The ghost glared back. Malcolm thought it was pretty good glaring. Cocoa didn't even glare that well. He wiped at the nozzle some more.

The staring contest went on a long time, but finally the ghost drooped. "You made

everything different. As soon as I was gone, you forgot about me."

Miss Nan's mouth hung open. "That's not true."

"Then why is everything different?" the ghost wailed.

"Because I'm trying to be like you," Miss Nan wailed back.

"Huh?" Malcolm said. If there was one thing he never tried to do, it was be like his sister. That was just crazy talk.

"I don't understand," the ghost said.

"That makes two of us," Malcolm muttered.

"Hush," Cocoa said, flapping a hand at Malcolm. "This is sister stuff."

"You always figured out what we should do whenever there was a problem," Miss Nan said. "That's what I'm trying to do."

The ghost narrowed her eyes. "How does chewing gum fix a problem?"

"The dancers were having trouble with rhythm," Miss Nan said. "They count, but it's not enough. When they chew gum, they chew with the rhythm of the music. And they dance better. By the time of the recital, they don't need the gum anymore."

"It works too," Cocoa shouted. "We're much better now."

"Wow," Malcolm said. "They must have been really terrible."

Cocoa turned to growl at him.

"What? I was trying to help."

"Fine," the ghost said. "Why let them sit in the padded seats?"

"Because this is an old theater," Miss Nan said. "The wooden stage has splinters." She took a step closer to her sister. "Don't

you remember? That's why we had those rules in the first place. You came up with them to solve problems."

"I do remember," the ghost said. She looked at her sister for a long moment before speaking again. "You remember too."

"I do. I remember when all you cared about was helping the dancers," Miss Nan said. "These pranks aren't helping them."

"They really aren't," Cocoa said.

The ghost didn't pay her any attention. Instead she floated over to Malcolm. "You can zap me now. I deserve it. I ruined everything."

"No," Miss Nan said. "Don't zap my sister."

"I'm not going to zap her," Malcolm said. "I think I have the perfect idea. I know exactly what you both need to do."

"What?" Miss Nan and the ghost asked at the same time.

"You go back to teaching together."

"How can we do that?" Miss Nan asked. "Parents won't let their children be taught by a ghost."

"Mom might," Cocoa said. "If we got a discount."

"Not helping." Malcolm turned to the teachers. "You can be Miss Nan and Miss Penny. Miss Penny can be a hologram that helps you. The parents already believe it. You just have to stop fighting."

"Good luck with that," Cocoa muttered.

"We could try that," Miss Nan suggested. "I could use the help. We're way behind."

"I would like to help," the ghost said.

"Even with the noisy dancing boys?" Miss Nan asked.

Miss Penny smiled. "Even with them."

Both of the dance teachers smiled at Malcolm. "Noisy boy," Miss Penny said. "Go and get the dancers. We have so much work to do."

"Will do!" Malcolm said, feeling pretty good about his idea. As he walked by Cocoa, she didn't even punch him.

On the night of the recital, Malcolm pushed Grandma Eunice down the aisle. He could see Miss Nan in the stage wings. Her ghostly sister stood by her. They both waved, then held up a finger to shush him.

"I'm not a noisy boy," he grumbled.

"Shush," Mom said. "Here's our spot."

Grandma Eunice poked Malcolm. "These recitals can last forever. You best go get me a snack at the concession stand. I could use some cheese puffs."

"That might not be a good idea," Malcolm said. He lowered his voice to a whisper. "I think Miss Penny is allergic."

"Fine, pork rinds then," Grandma Eunice said. "I can't make it through all the dancing without some kind of snack." She started to wheel her chair into the aisle. "Never mind. I'll go pick something out."

Mom hopped up and grabbed the wheelchair. "I'm sure Malcolm can get you one." She looked at him desperately. "Go get your grandmother a snack. Something that doesn't make too much noise."

"Fine."

Malcolm headed out to the concession stand. The line was long. With a sigh, he trudged to the end. Suddenly someone grabbed him by the scruff of the neck and dragged him down the hall.

"Hey!" Malcolm yelped, squirming to see who had hold of him. "Let go."

"Quiet!"

Malcolm recognized that voice. "Cocoa, what do you want?"

"I just wanted to say thanks. You're not the worst brother in the world." She narrowed her eyes. "But if you tell anyone I said that, I will clobber you."

She let him go and ran back to the stage door. Malcolm watched the door open and Miss Penny usher Cocoa inside.

"Sisters are weird," he muttered, but he had to admit, he felt good. Really good.

Questions for You

From Ghost Detectors
Malcolm and Dandy

Dandy: My love of cheese puffs gave Malcolm his big idea. Still, I got left out at the end, and that stinks. Have you ever been left out? How did you deal with that?

Malcolm: My laboratory still reeks of Cocoa's lip gloss! Have you ever had to share your space with someone else? How did you work that out?

Dandy: Those two dance teachers fought even more than Malcolm and Cocoa. Do you have anyone in your life who makes you mad like that? What do you do about it?

Malcolm: It looks like Grandma Eunice is going to be our Ghost Detector Support Staff forever. What if she was your grandmother? Would you let her be a Ghost Detector?